Dad's Favourite Newspaper

Dad's Favourite Newspaper

Azhagiyasingar

Translated from the Tamil by Aswini Kumar

ZERO DEGREE PUBLISHING

Original in Tamil, *Azhagiyasingar Sirukathaigal*: © Azhagiyasingar
English Translation, Dad's Favourite Newspaper : Aswini Kumar

First Edition by ZERO DEGREE PUBLISHING : November 2020
ISBN: 978-93-90053-09-4
ZDP Title : 34

ZERO DEGREE PUBLISHING
No.55(7), R Block, 6th Avenue,
Anna Nagar,
Chennai - 600 040

Website: www.zerodegreepublishing.com
E Mail id: zerodegreepublishing@gmail.com
Phone : 98400 65000

Typeset by Vidhya Velayudham
Cover Art by Aditya R

Contents

The Key

Krishnamurthy got ready for work in a rush. He had an unexpected problem to surmount that day. He had received a letter from a school asking Mano to appear for a test at1.30 that afternoon for admission into their Lower Kindergarten (LKG) class. The school was some three kilometres from his house. It was a very prestigious establishment and to claim his son was a student there was too big a deal to pass up on. Of course, it charged an arm and a leg for the privilege. Vijaya however was not too keen on Mano attending that school. Her main concern was his having to travel three kilometres to the school and back on his own every day. But Krishnamurthy was worried that unless Mano got an entry into the school this year, he might be hard-pressed to gain admission into the Upper KG class the next year. Vijaya, on the other hand, wished her son to be with her for at least one more year. Since she also went off to work, there would be no one to ensure Mano got off to school correctly and on time. Vijaya's mother was at her son's house, taking care of his children, and she had been asking for Mano to be sent there also so she could look after him and send him to school from her son's place.

As far as Krishnamurthy was concerned, he had no one other than his wife and son. As the elders in his family disappeared one after the other, he sometimes felt that they were being replaced by someone new every time. Mano's schooling had always been a bone of contention between the couple and the cause for Vijaya to frequently lose her temper. Since he had got to understand her very well within a few years of their marriage, Krishnamurthy did not mind the sharpness of her tongue and put it down to her innate nature.

"Now, now, be calm. Don't lose your patience. It will only increase your blood pressure and lead to heart problems."

"I'd welcome those conditions any day. Maybe they will help take me away from this earth faster."

"But, what will Mano and I do without you?"

"Marry another woman. Go ahead. You need someone all the time," she replied abruptly. That was her short way when angry, and he secretly enjoyed her snappy comebacks.

"Today is the interview at the school. Why shouldn't he appear for it?' he asked determinedly.

"I don't like it and I refuse to take a day off for this purpose."

"You carry on. I'll manage it myself somehow."

He had dropped Mano off at the crèche before proceeding to his workplace. Some days were busier than others at the office where he was employed as a stenographer. On that particular day he had assured his boss that he would complete a detailed report for which their head office had been clamouring for some time. He somehow needed to finish the report urgently that very day.

He entered the manager's office wondering how best to deal with the situation. His manager was already at work. This official was well over fifty years of age, with greying hair, but, as ever, very neatly dressed and sharp and energetic in his approach.

He looked up enquiringly at Krishnamurthy, who silently handed him the letter from the school. Having read it, he said, "You may leave at 12 and come back at 3.00."

"Thank you, sir. I'll be back by 3.00 and ensure the report is finished today itself, however long it takes," said Krishnamurthy gratefully.

He felt relieved as he headed towards his seat for he did not expect the problem to be resolved so smoothly. He had mentally anticipated having to take the day off. In all, there were a total of six employees in his office, including the manager. There was a female typist and three other officers in addition.

It was nearing 10.00 when Balakrishnan, one of the officers, entered the premises. When you thought of him the first thing to come to mind was his bushy moustache and he was therefore more commonly referred to as "handlebar Balakrishnan" by some of his colleagues. Krishnamurthy explained his predicament to him and requested, "Let me have the keys to the cupboard."

"What key? I don't have it," responded Balakrishnan.

Krishnamurthy was thrown for a moment for that meant he could not carry out any work till the afternoon. The two other officials had gone out on official business and both of them had keys to the office cupboard. It was obvious they had both carried away their keys with them through force of habit absentmindedly, instead of entrusting at least one to Balakrishnan. One of them was due to return to work in the afternoon while the other was away the whole day and would report for duty only the next morning. Since Krishnamurthy knew where the first official had gone, he called him up on the telephone. Yes, he had the key with him, but no, he was not in a position to return to the office to bring it back.

"What am I supposed to do?" he asked.

"Come here and get it. Borrow a scooter from someone in the office and get over here," he suggested.

"Who'd lend me their scooter? I do not like to ask for it, either," said Krishnamurthy.

"I just can't get back now. If you need the key, you'll have to come and get it," replied the officer and disconnected.

Krishnamurthy explained the position to Balakrishnan and asked him, "What do I do now?"

"Go and get the key," he suggested.

"Let me inform the Manager and leave," he said and went into the manager's room for the second time that day.

"Sir..."

The manager looked up at him.

"The cupboard keys are with Ravi and Venu..."

Before the manager could ask or say anything, a visitor entered the room and Krishnamurthy had no choice but to leave the place. He returned to his seat and sat down heavily in his chair wondering what on earth he would do now.

"Don't you always have a bunch of keys with you?" he tried once again with Balakrishnan.

"No. Ravi and Venu are the ones holding the keys normally," he replied.

The visitor had still not left the manager's room. Krishnamurthy looked out of the window at the neighbouring office building. A pair of doves were billing and cooing on one of the ledges conveniently situated for such an activity.

He could not sit still at his seat. The thought of the lengthy report haunted him. The computer floppy with all the data needed for the report was inside the cupboard. He still needed to get it out, open up the file, correct any errors and compile the elaborate report. Jayanthi, the other typist, had not yet turned up. The thought of Jayanthi reminded him of her lips, for she was constantly colouring her lips at work. Sometimes he also turned up late for work, just like her, but the manager was unaware of such transgressions for no one in the office was in the habit of snitching on their colleagues. The manager used to get upset only when his personal assistant, Ravi, landed up late for work.

The visitor at last came out of the manager's room and, with a slight smile at Krishnamurthy, left the premises.

He re-entered the manager's room.

"Sir..."

He looked up.

"The cupboard keys are with the two of them. May I go and get one of them from Venu?"

He seemed to have disregarded one fact when he said this.

"Are you waiting for me to go and get the key? Do whatever you want...take the day off or go and sit quietly at your desk...just don't stand here in my presence," he yelled.

Krishnamurthy was clueless and wondered what he had done to justify this outburst. But he did remove himself smartly from the manager's presence.

Balakrishnan looked at him and asked, "What did he say?"

"I should probably take the day off. He was needlessly angry with me," he replied.

"No, no. Go and get the key from Venu. Don't take his words to heart."

He stood there unsure of what to do.

"Do you have cash on you?"

"I have a hundred rupee note."

"That won't do. Here, take this twenty rupees. The auto-rickshaw driver will not have change for a hundred rupees so early in the morning," so saying he thrust two ten rupee notes on him. Silently he accepted them and walked away.

When he returned to the office after collecting the key from Venu, he was still feeling unnerved. Jayanthi had come in to work by then.

He quickly opened the cupboard and collected the materials he needed to finish his report.

By 12.00 mid-day, Venu also returned to the office but, in his upset state of mind, Krishnamurthy did not feel like chatting with any of them. At 12.30, he took his leave of them and left the office without going in to see the manager once again.

As he rode the local train back home, he kept ruing his lot in life and wondering why he was being afflicted with all these tribulations. He collected Mano from his crèche and took him to the school. It was an impressive place with enormous playground facilities and imposing buildings. There were several parents with their wards all with the same mission. He sat Mano down and once again took him through his paces, coaching him on how to respond to the Principal's queries. In view of the large student population, the school was operating in three shifts like a factory.

A teacher took Mano into a room where a team grilled him. They professed themselves satisfied at the end of the session. Then Krishnamurthy too was questioned and they announced that Mano would receive his admission notice by mail within the next few days. By the time the two of them left the school, it was past 3.00 p.m. and he felt there was no point in returning to work so late. He did not feel like going back either. It would have been better if he had taken the day off in the first instance. He called the office and spoke to Balakrishnan who answered the phone and told him of his inability to return to work that day. Balakrishnan assured him he would inform the manager of the situation.

He brought Mano back home. It was still very hot. It would still be some more time before Vijaya returned home. Now that Mano's admission had been assured, he needed to raise the necessary cash for the school fees. From now on, an argument would erupt every morning before the two of them left for their offices. After sending the child off to school, he would sit and worry about him all day at the office.

When he entered the house, he found the maid, Prema, already there busily washing the morning's dishes. Krishnamurthy had always found her a very hardworking woman. She was a widow with three children – two daughters and a son, about Mano's age.

He heated up some milk and mixed himself a cup of coffee. As he was sipping it, Prema came and stood before him with tears in her eyes, wiping her wet hands on her *sari*. She had apparently finished her work for the day fairly quickly.

"Why are you crying?"

"I have lost my house keys."

"House keys?"

"Yes, and I cannot get into my house without it."

"Where did you lose it?"

"I always keep it on this ledge by the window. I think Mano must have thrown it away somewhere."

And Prema kept on crying.

"Hold on. Stop crying. If you cannot trace the key, perhaps the lock can be broken open. But, first, look carefully everywhere once again. The key must be somewhere around."

"I have looked everywhere. I usually keep it on the ledge by this window."

He went and looked around the window area but could not find the key anywhere.

"You shouldn't have kept it there where everyone can see it...Mano, come here...did you take Prema's house key?"

Mano simply gave a mischievous smile without answering the question.

"Did you?"

Mano shook his head in such a way it was impossible to judge whether he did or did not.

"Answer me. Did you take it or not?"

"No."

"Don't lie to me..."

"Yes, I did...No...no...I don't know anything... dad, I was simply..."

"Where did you put it? Show me."

"I won't get it for you. Go, look for it yourself."

Krishnamurthy was instantly reminded of his manager's unreasonable outburst at him that morning. Mano nonchalantly ran off to swing on the compound gate.

———

(1994)

Hello uncle!

We found our seats on the Brindavan Express just as the train started steaming out of the station. I was in a foul mood and behaved as though we were two total strangers occupying adjacent seats for the duration of a journey. But, even though I was extremely upset with her, I did not verbalise it by ranting and raving. That was not in my nature. I let my thoughts float on waves of anger but did not express them aloud to her. It was indeed a strange state of affairs. The relationship we had built up over the past several years and the affectionate ties we had developed as a result were the ones now preventing me from openly expressing my feelings to her. She gestures and mutters, "Why? Why?" I deliberately draw away and convey my rage through my eyes alone. She asks for coffee and I pretend not to hear her. She does not understand

and looks at me uncomprehendingly. No, no, she gets it. I am certain she feels confident we will get over this crisis also soon enough.

"Relax. Why do you worry unnecessarily? They'll take good care of him."

"Forget it. You don't have any affection towards him."

"But what's the alternative?'

"Why don't you take time off work?"

"I don't have any more vacation days left. In any case, they will look after him better than I do."

"How can you say that? Aren't you his mother?"

She kept quiet. I too held my tongue as my anger would have boiled over and my language deteriorated had the discussion continued.

How can she abandon the child and move on? As a mother, she was expected to have more love and attachment towards him than me. How then has she hardened her heart and accepted the current situation? I just didn't get it. If there was a debate on who loved a child more, the father or the mother, she appeared to be a eloquent spokesperson for the fathers' side. In my frustrated state of mind, such a debate and the kind of crowd that would enjoy it flashed before my mind's eye and tormented me.

As the train gathered speed, my thoughts also galloped along. It surprised me that I was able to think of her as a stranger I did not recognise. Even though she was right next to me, I felt I did not know her at all. With that thought a kind shyness, which is brought on when a strange girl is seated next to you, enveloped me. When she glanced at me, it felt alien and I deliberately suppressed the angry words that rose to my lips. She understood my state of mind and held her peace.

A few hours ago, Shyam was holding on to the bars of the window staring out at the street outside. I stood out of his sight, gazing at him.

When it had been decided to leave him behind in his aunt's place, the thought that we would see him next only after a gap of a few months was eating at me. I didn't think it right to oppose the move then as her mother and sister were adamant about the details of the arrangement. Her sister was eagerly looking forward to having him stay with them for the next few months and the thought that the value of a child was more keenly appreciated by the childless sister kept me from demolishing her happiness.

She did not provide me with an opportunity to speak my mind. If she had, I would have opposed the move and nipped it in the bud itself. She was in the habit of deciding upon such matters herself probably because she did not consider it such a big deal. Am I blowing the issue up out of proportion? Why should I take this issue so emotionally? There was no doubt they would take good care of him; so, why should I worry my head so much?

When we left the house, we made sure Shyam did not glimpse our exit through the window. Had he seen us leave, he might have ended up creating a scene.

It was only when we reached Bangalore bus stand that I felt the full torment of Shyam's memory, her role in the whole scenario and my own dormant impotence. The more I thought about it, the angrier I grew.

Even after we reached Chennai, we alighted from the train as though we were complete strangers. While she followed me like a shadow, we avoided any form of communication. We went across the road to the bus stop opposite the railway station to await our bus. Various buses kept passing by. The smell from the hospital next to the bus stop and the pervading atmosphere of pestilence was disgusting. The nurses in their whites wore a deadened, mechanical look.

Our bus finally arrived. In spite of my anger, I watched to see if she got on safely. Perhaps I was worried that, in response to my unspoken anger, she would react equally angrily herself, and refuse to accompany me on the bus. In any case, we both got on in our listless state of mind. And when we got off I found that I had lost my wallet. I chalked up the loss to my angry state of mind. Boiling with anger, I had let my attention wander and had been unaware of what was happening around me.

After a few days, my anger dissipated and we started behaving normally. I felt slightly ashamed at myself for having needlessly lost my temper. It appeared that she had been returned to me after my anger had vanished. I thought back to the moments when we had behaved shamelessly together and they gave me additional happiness. Time went by, the child was forgotten and we were together again.

A few months later, the two of us proceeded once again to Bangalore to bring the child and my wife's mother back with us to Chennai. I was brimming with anticipation this time and, as I looked at her seated next to me on the train, I felt proud and possessive. She seemed like a precious object that belonged only to me. Halfway through the journey, she dozed off leaning against my shoulder. That is the way she likes to nap during trips and I like it too.

As soon as entered her sister's house, she picked up Shyam and started kissing and cuddling him. I looked at the boy carefully. His complexion had not changed but he appeared to have lost some weight. When I remarked on this, I was told that he had just recovered from a slight fever.

I extended my hands towards him to take him in my arms. He appeared hesitant.

He did not exhibit the same freedom with me as he did with his mother. I tried my best to divert him and, even though he enjoyed all my efforts from afar, he still did not approach me. When I tried pulling him towards me, he resisted and began snivelling. I looked at her angrily at this behaviour. She tried to pacify me. Her mother came up with an explanation, "It's been some time since he last saw you. He probably does not recognise you. Give him some time." The child's reaction must have secretly provoked laughter among them. I felt like I needed to get away from there straightaway. But I didn't do so, thinking it would be tantamount to insulting them. Plus, they had been looking after the child for so many months while I had abandoned him there out of compulsion. In the circumstances, any display of anger would not be proper. Shyam seemed to be shy around me while they kept urging him to go to me and greet me. In my state of mind, even this attempt on their part seemed derisory and felt like they were indirectly poking fun at me in order to satisfy their own egos. Then, impelled by their urgings, Shyam slowly neared me. He hesitated for a while, then slowly looked up at me and greeted me. "Hello, uncle," he said.

(1997)

The Pink Shirt

Saraswathy pedalled her cycle furiously. She needed to deliver two lunch boxes – one small and one large – urgently to Padmanabhan before he left for work in the mornings. These boxes contained his breakfast and lunch for the day, and it was her responsibility to ensure they reached him early in the morning every day. Saraswathy found this a challenge on a daily basis. Preparing two meals, packing them in lunch boxes and delivering them on time early every morning was no mean feat. In the same manner, Mr. Padmanabhan found getting ready for work each day a daunting proposition.

Saraswathy arrived at Padmanabhan's apartment in a rush.

"I was waiting for you all this while," remarked Padmanabhan.

"I came as quickly as I could," she replied.

Padmanabhan looked at her with some compassion. At the same time, her looks never ceased to amaze him. She was taller than an average woman, and used to comment, "The stairs in your house are too narrow. I also need to duck so as not to hit my head on the lintel." He had to resist the urge to give her a big hug.

He would collect the two boxes from Saraswathy and sprint as though he was running the second leg of a relay race. At such moments, he would ask himself the purpose of this life and come up with the answer "to keep running", and laugh at the absurdity of it all. Saraswathy was running frantically in her life, and Padmanabhan was racing perennially in his.

Next he had to catch the bus to his workplace. If he missed the usual one, it would be past 10 by the time he reached his office. The bank would then be filled with irate customers and he would walk into a scene of mayhem. On very rare occasions, the place would be deserted and echoing.

Padmanabhan managed to get on the usual bus and even secured a seat at the rear. It was only then that he realised he was wearing his jinxed pink shirt. God, oh God, there was certain to be some unpleasant argy-bargy at work that day and he was sure to have to weather a rough day.

On a Sunday, when he had gone to Chennai as was customary, he and his wife had visited a popular clothing shop where he had picked up three shirts of the same design in different colours. When he had worn them to work one after the other, the pink shirt had caused him problems right from the very first day he had worn it.

He had had a fight with V. R. Ramakrishnan on that fateful day. It was a busy day at the bank and customers kept streaming in even after normal banking hours. One of them, requiring a Demand Draft urgently, had come up to Padmanabhan and importuned him, "Sir, it is the last day today." "You should have come in earlier," he responded, but took him to V.R. Ramakrishnan to plead his case (VRR was looking after cash and was also in charge of issuing Demand Drafts), "Sir, this gentleman requires an urgent DD." VRR grabbed that excuse to yell at the top of his voice, "Look, how much cash is lying uncounted...where's the time for me...?"

"Just one DD, sir. Apparently it's the last date today."

"Impossible, sir. I am calling up the Circle Office straightaway. It's a heavy cash day, in addition to being a Saturday..." VRR had yelled.

Frustrated, Padmanabhan went back to his seat. He was well aware that VRR would not let the matter rest. He would insist upon blowing it out of all proportion. The problem was everyone in the branch was used to acquiesce to him.

The customer too was fed up at the lack of service.

"Do you have money in your account here? If so, I can arrange for a DD immediately," offered Padmanabhan.

"No sir," he replied. Having no other option, he went on his way disappointed.

Padmanabhan was disgusted at VRR for using this incident to create a scene. Generally speaking, he did not care for persons who shouted and acted like drama queens. In particular, VRR was a person who had double standards. At every monthly office meeting, he used to hold forth on the kind of customer service that he was in the habit of providing to the bank's clients. That Saturday, the Bank Manager was absent and Padmanabhan was officiating as the branch in-charge.

When he was proceeding as usual to Chennai that night, VRR's shouts kept echoing in his ears. He thought it was disrespectful on VRR's part not to have accepted cash from the customer and felt genuine personal regret at this lapse in service. It was while he was on the bus that he first paid attention to the shirt he was wearing and noticed that he was wearing the new pink shirt for the first time. He liked the shirt, but could not help but wonder if the colour had offended VRR somehow and affected his mood. That was the first time when Padmanabhan began relating the colour of his shirt to happenings at the office.

That was also when he noticed another fact: every time he wore the pink shirt to the bank, there was certain to be an unnecessary kerfuffle at the workplace. The problem however was limited only to the workplace; he never had any problem elsewhere while wearing that shirt. He did not come to this conclusion in a hurry either.

The next time he wore the pink shirt to the bank, another misunderstanding had resulted. A middle-aged woman customer, who had come to withdraw cash, had mistaken him and it had taken all his diplomatic skills to calm her down. Padmanabhan was examining the lady's account to ascertain the source of her funds and had asked this question to the person in the bank in charge of the savings bank accounts. On hearing the question, the lady customer had mistakenly interpreted it to mean that Padmanabhan was referring to her as a thief and kicked up a massive row. She had also called up her husband to back her up, and it was all Padmanabhan could do to calm the two of them down and explain himself to their grudging satisfaction.

Another unforgettable incident – featuring the same pink shirt.

It was after this episode that Padmanabhan started feeling that it was difficult to read and understand not only his colleagues but also the bank's customers. He would then start philosophising, what's life, what's the meaning of life, and so on.

Perhaps if he had been in Chennai, he would not have to ponder on all these tricky metaphysical questions?

Every time he wore that accursed shirt thereafter, it was an almost unconscious action. It was the same case on the day he needed to transmit quick data urgently and he had requested Sundaresan to attend to the matter as a matter of priority. Sundaresan was a 30-year old bachelor who was very keen on women. In spite of his urgent assignment, he initiated a conversation with a lady customer and went on chatting with her for hours. Padmanabhan lost his patience.

"Sundaresan," he called out.

Sundaresan pretended not to hear him.

After a little while, Padmanabhan called out to him again. The lady customer heard him this time. Padmanabhan noticed her perky breasts thrusting out provocatively. She looked at him apprehensively, but Sundaresan went on chatting with her unconcernedly, staring at her all the while.

Padmanabhan felt frustrated and decided there was no point hailing Sundaresan again. In due course, Sundaresan escorted that lady to the door of the bank and bade her goodbye.

He then came straight to Padmanabhan's seat.

"What sort of behaviour is that? I was chatting with a customer and you kept calling out to me very rudely?"

"As far as I am concerned, office work is more important than chatting with customers," replied Padmanabhan. At that, Sundaresan started shouting, repeating himself again and again as though that made everything all right.

Padmanabhan soon realised that there was no point in arguing with him. The quick data that was supposed to be transmitted that day did not go and when asked for an explanation, Sundaresan merely said, "There was a rush of customers today and I could not attend to it." That is when Padmanabhan noticed he had his pink shirt on.

The same thought again struck him – that the shirt was the cause of all the troubles. As soon as he reached home, he took it off and threw it in a corner.

His belief that something always went wrong every time he wore that shirt to work was strengthened. "Let me get it out of sight," he thought but did not have the mind to give it away.

It was the only shirt in his wardrobe that actually attracted him and he had also noticed that if he wore it to other places, nothing bad resulted. He tried telling himself it was only a figment of his overactive imagination, but that didn't help either.

He had avoided the shirt for several days thereafter.

***

Today, while seated in the bus, his thoughts reverted to the pink shirt. How did he happen to select the shirt today, he wondered. Was it because he had let his laundry pile up throughout the week? Was it the only clean shirt in his wardrobe?

It was the month-end and the day when accounts had to be closed at the bank. Everything depended on the computers functioning normally and all the staff cooperating.

Padmanabhan tried to calm himself down saying, "Take a deep breath. Don't get flustered," mentally to himself.

When he entered the bank, there was already a larger than usual crowd waiting to be served.

The manager's room was also packed full of people. Knowing the manager's temperament, Padmanabhan expected him to lose his cool and explode at any moment. As anticipated, an event took place.

A non-resident Indian had come in to check his balance in the bank's system and open a fresh deposit utilising the amount at his credit.

The manager summoned Padmanabhan and instructed him to attend to the customer's needs and stipulated the transaction should be completed in ten minutes' time.

His flustered manner only increased Padmanabhan's tension. He was certain the manager would appear before him in exactly ten minutes demanding the receipt.

Padmanabhan approached Madhavan, who handled deposits, and requested him to do the needful urgently. Madhavan was a 58-year young man and was finding it impossible to cope with the crowd that day. He took the paper handed by Padmanabhan and tossed it into a corner of his desk.

Padmanabhan again called Madhavan and chivvied him, "Please complete this transaction quickly, the party is waiting."

When Madhavan completed the paperwork, the bank's computer crashed.

Padmanabhan's tension only grew as he expected the manager to appear before him at any moment to ask about the transaction.

Madhavan could do nothing further and he gave up trying. The bank continued to teem with customers.

As expected, the manager appeared. "Where's the receipt, Padmanabhan?" he enquired.

"A small problem, sir..." began Padmanabhan.

"I don't want to hear anything. I've told you he's an important client and he's been waiting for some time now. I need it done quickly," the manager began screaming.

"We'll set the problem right very soon, sir," soothingly explained Padmanabhan.

"See to it," and the manager left.

Padmanabhan went over to Madhavan's seat in agitation.

He was not at all surprised to hear that the computer had acted up that day.

He collected the papers from Madhavan and gave them to VRR, who was a computer whiz. Luckily, VRR was in a good mood and was not officiating as the Chief Cashier that day. Somehow, he overrode the problem and had the receipt printed out.

By the time Padmanabhan took the receipt to the manager's room, an hour had passed, and the manager ungraciously snatched the receipt from his hand while directing a glare at him.

Padmanabhan came back to his seat and sat down with a sigh. Pondering over the day's events, he happened to glance at his shirt.

"At it again, pink shirt?" he told himself.

It only got worse as the day wore on. The computer continued to act up and they could not close that day's accounts. Padmanabhan wondered what could be done to rectify the situation caused by an error on Madhavan's part.

He asked Madhavan to stay back awhile and complete the day's tallying of accounts. Madhavan not only refused the request outright, but also went to the manager and complained that Padmanabhan was asking him to stay back after working hours.

Padmanabhan was confused as to his course of action.

On hearing Madhavan's complaint, the manager came rushing up to Padmanabhan and asked him angrily, "Why are you asking Madhavan to stay back? He can't as he's only an award staff. You're the systems manager. Do something."

The computer system would not allow them to close the day's accounts.

He once again called Madhavan and requested, "Madhavan, just cancel the entry you made. That should do for the time being. Please stay back a short while to do that at least."

"No, you heard the manager. I am not supposed to stay," said Madhavan angrily and again went to the manager's room to complain.

Padmanabhan braced himself for a fresh onslaught from the manager.

As expected, the manager pounced on him, like a tiger released from its confines, and his angry screams rattled the entire building this time. A few customers who were still at the premises were shocked at his behaviour.

Padmanabhan felt highly insulted at this treatment. It was no use trying to explain matters to the manager for he was not in a receptive frame of mind. Neither did he possess enough intelligence to understand the problem with the computers. Padmanabhan wondered why the manager was targeting him instead of asking Madhavan to stay back for a short while to carry out the necessary entries.

The manager's angry tirade wounded Padmanabhan deeply. Never before in his life had anyone spoken to him in this manner. Not once had his 84-year old father scolded him, and neither his wife nor his friends had ever used such words against him.

He could not accept the fact that being a workplace, the manager had vented at him, using him as a punching bag, upset at something that had gone wrong at work, and let it go at that.

He could have shouted back at the manager, but it was not in his character to do so. If he attempted to raise his voice, his entire body would shiver with rage and the end result would have been disastrous. He was not in a position to put forth his justifications cogently and when someone blasted him, all he could do was to take it.

He did not bother Madhavan thereafter. He called up the Systems In-Charge at his Regional Office who set the problem right within a few minutes. In the process, he also managed to understand the root of the glitch.

Tired and wrung-out, he reached Saraswathy's house that evening to collect his supper.

Her children were waiting for her outside their house.

The younger boy was buck naked. When he saw him, the older boy ran in and brought out Padmanabhan's packed supper and handed it to him saying, "Mother said you'd come around." As he collected it and was turning away, Saraswathy made her appearance on her bicycle.

"You're returning home only now?" asked Padmanabhan admiring her industry.

"Yes, sir. This is the boy who is unwell. He seems to have a problem passing urine normally," she said.

When he looked at the boys again, Padmanabhan felt sorry for them. Both were so young and innocent.

He started from the place with his own heavy heart. Every time he looked at Saraswathy, he would feel like striking up a conversation with her. She had such attractive features.

"Sir," said Saraswathy.

Padmanabhan looked back at her enquiringly.

"This shirt suits you very well, sir. It matches your complexion also," said Saraswathy.

Padmanabhan was surprised at the comment. "Really?" he asked.

Latterly, he has stopped wearing the pink shirt, especially to his workplace. For a considerable period of time he kept thinking about persons who cause hurt to others through their words. Who do you pity or feel compassionate towards? The one who hurts others? Or, the person who is injured?

He has not yet been able to find an answer to this question.

———

The Byroad

The byroad has remained the same as long as anyone can remember, except that it has become a bit more crowded. The main road is within walking distance from it, and you can catch buses from there to all parts of the city. The railway station is a mere 2 kilometres away. The main road presents an impressive appearance, teeming with vehicles and resounding with their cacophony.

Ever since Shanmugam moved in there, the normally dirty street was transformed into an extraordinarily filthy one. Shanmugam was in the milk business and, when he took up his residence in the alley, he came accompanied by four or five milch cows. Currently he owns some eight or nine of these animals and the cows have also become permanent residents of the street along with us humans. There would always be a few flicking their tails contemptuously at passersby, while others would lounge languidly in the gutters that ran on both sides of the alleyway. It was sometimes difficult to make out the buffaloes in the muddy waters of the drains.

The byroad was not officially recognised by the City Corporation. It had open running drains on both sides throughout its length. In the section where Shanmugam resided, thanks to his cows, the water from the drains would accumulate in front of the houses, and their residents suffered horrendously from the mosquitoes that bred prolifically in the stagnant waters.

Having mulled over various proposals for bettering the lot of the alley, we formed a 'Welfare Association' with Raman as its Secretary. We would hold meetings whenever he felt like it, on the terrace of his house. But not all members of the Association would turn up at these meetings. Raman was a retired government servant.

In the initial days following his appointment as Secretary, Raman's voice could be heard blaring throughout the alley. He would shout at everyone on the street. Some of the young boys were in the habit of defecating by the side of the lane, next to the drains. A few householders would dump their garbage on the street near the dumpsters. No one paid much heed to his bellowing, but some of the youngsters would hurriedly run back home before they completed their business on the street.

The first order of business of the Welfare Association was Shanmugam's cows, and Raman had taken this issue up with him as soon as he first moved in to the lane. Very humbly, Shanmugam requested that he be given a few months' breather by which time he hoped to move elsewhere with his herd. Raman was ecstatic at the belief that the problem had been sorted out. Shanmugam merely used the respite to extend his few months' tenure into several years' and, by the clever stratagem of marrying his landlord's daughter, altered his status from that of a tenant to one of a permanent resident of the lane. This was a big blow to Raman and he stopped raising Shanmugam's issue in front of other members.

Slowly, the noise level on the street also increased day by day. The youngsters included the alley's gutters in their daily games of marbles, cricket, spinning tops and others. In the ensuing battles, one child or the other was sure to end up caterwauling.

During the rainy seasons, the cows on the street posed a problem to everyone.

Vadivu kept complaining about Shanmugam to anyone who would listen. She had made her pile in the illicit hooch business and was well-known to all the policemen in the vicinity. She had a tender heart and would cry buckets while watching tragic Tamil movies, but when it came to a war of words, no one could match her vocabulary of obscene cuss words. Fearing her foul mouth, not many would dare tangle with her, but Shanmugam had once not only taken her on but also bested her. Ever since, Vadivu made sure she stayed clear of Shanmugam.

The street was shaped like a "U". There was only one path to the main road. As it was a narrow lane, it culminated in a tall wall at one end. Across that wall was another street backing on to the houses situated there. During the rains, all of us took a shortcut through a bylane adjoining Vadivu's house to gain access to the main road. While her house was located in our street, the bylane adjacent to it led directly to the main road, and we did not therefore have to traverse the entire length of our street for this purpose. This was a commonly accepted practice for all of us to avoid Shanmugam's cows, but following her altercation with him she did something that totally severed her connection with our street. She fenced off the bylane next to her house, erected a gate in it and locked it up so that the residents of the street had no alternative but to go through the cow-infested street to get to the main road.

Since it was not acknowledged by the Corporation, the street was not paved. There were no storm water drains and no street lights.

It was just when we had given up all hope that the lane would ever see better days that the news of the upcoming elections renewed our expectations.

For many years now, the constituency which comprised our street had been the stronghold of the opposition candidate. His grip was so tight that the area was considered an impregnable fortress by his party. I had not bothered to pay heed to all the election promises he would hurl from the stage during his campaign speeches for he had not even once bothered to come to our street seeking votes. His supporters were however very active in plastering every wall in the constituency with posters and hanging party buntings and flags everywhere. Our street was no exception and did not escape their attention either. The Member, as was his wont, did not bother putting in an appearance at our street this time around as well.

The ruling party candidate, however, proved he was no pushover. He did something the other fellow had never bothered to do: he came into our street himself and went from house to house introducing himself and reiterating his party's poll assurances. He even organised a street corner meeting in our lane where he did not fail to point out that the sitting Member had done nothing for the development of the constituency.

His words were music to our ears. Raman felt that this election was going to be an important milestone and he began hobnobbing with the candidate from the ruling party on a daily basis.

One evening, while returning home from work, I saw Raman seated on the dais with the ruling party candidate conducting an election rally. When he saw me staring at him, he gave me a sheepish smile and looked away self-consciously.

On poll day, everyone in the street went out and voted for the ruling party's candidate and he won, what was supposed to be the opposition's iron fortress, by a small margin. The ruling party came back to power.

Within a few days, some of their party workers went from house to house on our street, taking down our complaints in a notebook.

Raman was ecstatic. "Did the previous Member ever bother to do this? See? This man is taking note of all our complaints so he can take action," he went about telling everyone in the street.

All of us made the point about Shanmugam and the nuisance created by his cows in the Member's grievance book. In fact, Raman even led a delegation from our street to the new Member's office regarding this issue. As suggested by the Member, we also wrote out a complaint letter and gathered signatures from all the residents, and anxiously awaited the outcome of our efforts.

The cows continued to flick their tails imperiously at the passersby.

All this happened a year ago. Raman gave up approaching the Member in connection with our woes, as he had his own household problems to sort out. He also expressed his desire to step down from the position of Secretary of the Welfare Association to whoever would listen, but no one was willing to relieve him of the post. While the post carried no special perks, all the residents in the street actually needed his services. While it was true that he could not solve the issue of Shanmugam's cows, he was still useful in a number of sundry matters like complaining about electricity outages, collecting fees from each household and arranging for garbage pick-up and cleaning of the gutters, co-ordinating with the Corporation on civic issues etc. He even filed a case, on behalf of the welfare association, against the Corporation questioning their tax levies while providing no services at all to the residents of the street.

Whenever a small crowd congregated and talked politics, a few of them were sure to ask derisively, "What the hell has the new Member done for us?" just to watch Raman squirm.

Unable to put up with the nuisance caused by the cows much longer, one of the householders lodged a secret complaint with a nearby police station. Shanmugam thereafter became a regular contributor to the policemen's welfare fund.

One day I was proceeding on my cycle to attend wedding at a friend's place when I found a buffalo chewing its cud in the middle of the street completely blocking it. I could not get past it and was vainly attempting to make it to move by ringing my bicycle bell when Shanmugam's wife came out of her house truculently.

"Go and complain to anyone you like. Who can question us? Who here has the guts to take us on? We have now connections right to the top," she yelled while grudgingly moving the buffalo to one side. I was furious but knew that arguing with her was futile. So, I quietly pedalled away.

But I felt that this matter should be put to rest once and for all and proceeded to the Member's house. It was overflowing with people who had come to see him on one mission or the other, and I was asked to wait my turn. A short while later I was called in. The Member was surrounded by his party functionaries and some petitioners were seated in front of him.

He looked at me and asked the purpose of my visit. I mentioned the name of the street and added that I had come from there.

"Do you need a certificate?"

"No, no. That's not it."

"What's the matter then?"

"I need to talk to you about the street where I live."

"Go ahead."

"You know Mr. Raman..."

"Which Mr. Raman?"

I looked at him in astonishment. One of the men around him prompted, "You remember that Brahmin guy?"

"Oh, him? Yes, I know him," nodded the Member. His expression indicated he had caught on why I was there.

For my part, I recited the entire wretched history of the street. When I finished and looked at him, his mien did nothing to inspire any confidence in me.

"I'll certainly consider everything you have said. Bring me another petition and I shall take the necessary action," he said.

"They let the cows wander all over the street and they make a mess everywhere. It is intolerable."

"I'll certainly look into it. Come back with a petition."

I thanked him for form's sake and walked out. When I came out and looked around at the road he lived in, I saw a broad thoroughfare with trees on both sides providing shade and a touch of greenery to the location. The heat of the sun was hardly perceptible under the canopy of the overhanging boughs while colourful blooms lay strewn at the foot of the trees. The chirping of the birds added to the overall ambience of the setting.

(1991)

The Locker

Imust confess to a slight irritation when Mrs. Chari called me up that Saturday. The bank was supposed to close for business at 2.00 p.m. on Saturdays, after which we had to stay back to close and tally the accounts. It would be at least 3.00 by the time we would be able to leave the bank's premises, and it had been a constant grouse of mine that I could not afford to relax even on Saturdays.

Mrs. Chari currently resides in Nanganallur. It is just her and her husband now. Their children are scattered all over India and abroad, and every one of them is extremely well-settled in life. Mr.Chari himself had retired from a highly-placed position and was currently drawing a substantial pension. They used to live at Thiruvallikeni earlier and the account they had opened then at our branch was continuing till date. If they had wished, they could have shifted it to a bank nearer their residence at any time, but they did not do so. The reason: they considered our branch lucky for them, and Mrs. Chari would travel all the way from Nanganallur to operate her locker at our premises. She would scrutinise her bank accounts and query if any interest payments were delayed. She would go straight to our Chief Manager to complain of any lapse, and he would summon me to his room and ask for an explanation.

She would then come over to my seat and complain that her interest payments, due on the 1st of each month, were consistently delayed. It was my job to placate her and promise to do better in the future.

Gita, who was seated next to me in the office, would advise me, "Sir, handle the lady with care. Else, she would move all her deposits to another bank."

But Gita's assistance in this regard was confined solely to her verbal advice on how to handle Mrs. Chari. She would not offer to help in any matter, for it was not in her nature to sully her hands by doing any actual work.

Saturdays were always busy and, since it was the first week-end of the month, the branch was thronged.

Mrs. Chari landed up exactly at 1.30 p.m.

"Sorry, I'm late," she apologised.

"Please take a seat," I offered.

I then became busy attending to the customers already seated in front of me and forgot all about Mrs. Chari's presence.

It was only when Gita prompted, "Sir, please escort Mrs. Chari to the locker room," that I remembered the lady's existence.

I got her to sign the locker register and escorted her to where the lockers were located. Truth to tell, each trip to the locker room was a painful one for me as the lockers in our branch were situated in the basement of the building next to our strong-room.

I took her into the vault and opened her safe deposit box with my master key. She had on lease a large locker. Additionally, her sons and daughters also had lockers of their own at our bank. She had this habit of taking out each and every object in her locker and checking it off against a list in a notebook that she carried with her.

"Please finish quickly today, ma'am. It's a Saturday and we only work half a day. We'll be locking up shortly," I requested.

"Fine, fine," said Mrs. Chari.

I came back up to my seat panting slightly. Every time I had to negotiate the stairs I felt short of breath. This locker business was a huge nuisance. I would have escorted one customer down to the vaults and come up panting for breath only to find another client waiting to be led down to the basement. This was a continuous process throughout the day and it irritated me no end. But I kept the irritation bottled up within myself. I could hardly exhibit it to the customers, could I?

Another problem with the lockers was waiting for me when I came up from the vault. A well-dressed man was waiting to add his name to the locker register. I asked him to be seated and examined the piece of paper that he had brought with him.

"Whose name is the locker in currently?" I asked.

"It's in the joint names of my sister and her husband."

"They need to come personally for this purpose."

"But they are not in India. They are both in the US."

"They need to come here at least once personally and put in an application to add your name in the ledger."

"But they are not in a position to come immediately."

"I am sorry. In that case, I cannot help you."

"But here's the letter from them requesting that my name be added…"

"A mere letter won't do. They need to come personally to avoid any problems later."

Unhappy with my reply, he shouted at me in anger and left the bank.

Ours is a hundred year old bank and lockers have always been a source of friction with the customers.

As it was a Saturday, we were supposed to close all transactions by 12.00 noon. That was easier said than done with the kind of crowd that we were handling. Very slowly the crowd started dissipating and, with that, the staff members also started to leave one by one. Gita was, of course, one of the earliest to leave. Lucky girl! Her house was quite close to the workplace and she could afford to take it easy. Jagannathan, who handled savings accounts, also left to grab a quick bite.

The Chief Manager had a meeting to attend at the Regional Office in the morning, and had already left earlier in the day. As it was a Saturday, he would not be back. It was his usual habit to catch the Saturday night train to Bangalore, spend the weekend there, and return to work on Monday morning. The Loan Officer hailed from a distant suburb and, come Saturday, would disappear fairly early without informing anyone. The Chief

Manager and he had regular arguments on this issue.

Now, the gentleman handling pension payments has also locked up and is on his way out. The only ones left, apart from me, are the Chief Cashier and the peon Kesavan who stayed back to lug the heavy cash boxes and help me lock up.

The Chief Cashier hailed me.

"Sir, I'm done. Please come."

"Here," I entered the Chief Cashier's cubicle, counted everything and affixed my signature. Then I called Kesavan over and the three of us proceeded downstairs with Kesavan carrying the cash trunk. We entered the strong-room in the basement, opened it, stacked all the cash boxes inside and locked it after us using several keys. We then locked the door at the top of the staircase.

"What a busy day. And on top of it, there were a few counterfeit notes also to be dealt with," said the Cashier in frustration. And then he too took his leave.

It was then just me and Kesavan. It would some time to complete the accounts on the computer and I tried to work as fast as I could.

"Look at us Kesavan? Here we are, unable to get home quickly even on Saturdays," I remarked in vexation.

"That's true, sir," he agreed.

I could see he was itching to get away and start his drinking session, since it was a Saturday, after all.

"Is Jagannathan still around?"

"No, sir. He left long back. I thought you knew."

"Then let's lock up and go home."

Kesavan and I proceeded to lock up and leave. When he switched off the electricity mains, I thought I heard a faint cry from somewhere.

"Kesava, I thought I heard someone shouting from somewhere. Did you hear anything?"

"Sir, perhaps it was from outside, on the road. Let's go."

When I was locking the main gate to the bank I felt a faint sense of unease.

I reached home relieved that I did not have to give a thought about the bank for one whole day.

I leave home at West Mambalam for Thiruvallikeni at 8.00 every morning and by the time I return home again it would be 8:00 at night. The traffic on Anna Salai would be simply horrendous.

"You seem to have returned home early today?" remarked my wife.

"That's because the Chief Manager wasn't around when I left. If he had been there, he is sure to have delayed me."

"Let's go the vegetable market today. I'd like to buy the month's supplies today itself," said my wife.

"I'm feeling a little sleepy. Let me take a short nap. Wake me up when you are ready to go," I said and went into the bedroom.

I felt I had just dozed off when I seemed to hear someone moaning. I quickly woke up and looked at the clock. It was 6:00 p.m. I was suddenly reminded of Mrs. Chari and I remembered that I had not seen her coming out of the locker room. I dressed hurriedly and called Kesavan.

"Yes sir?" said Kesavan.

"Come to the office immediately. I do not remember Mrs. Chari leaving the bank premises. I have a horrible feeling we have locked her in."

"But I checked around, sir. There was no one about."

"No, I am feeling uneasy. Let's open the bank and check once again."

"What happened? Aren't we going shopping?"

"Not now," I answered irritatedly.

Once again I drove towards Thiruvallikeni. Mambalam was chock-a-block with shoppers. Throughout the way I kept praying to all the gods that Mrs. Chari should not be at the bank's premises.

On the way, I stopped by at the Chief Cashier's house and borrowed his set of keys. "What for?" he asked.

"I have a horrible feeling Mrs. Chari is locked in," I replied.

"Oh my God! Should I come along?"

"No. Don't bother. I'll bring the keys back when I'm done."

Kesavan was waiting for me at the bank's gates.

"Kesava, I have a feeling Mrs. Chari did not come out of the locker room and we have locked her in."

"How is it possible, sir? Doesn't she have a cell phone? Wouldn't she have called somebody for help?"

"I don't know the answers to these questions. Let's hurry."

We opened a series of doors and entered the premises. I switched on the mains. Kesavan hurried and opened the door to the staircase and switched the lights on.

A few rats were scurrying around and when they heard us approach, they quickly hid themselves.

"Sir, I can't hear any sound. Looks like it was all in your imagination."

We opened the strong-room. Once locked the place would be airtight and anyone stuck inside would asphyxiate and die in double quick time.

My heart stopped for a moment.

Yelling, "I am sorry, Mrs. Chari," I rushed into the locker room.

Mrs. Chari was lying unconscious on the floor.

I got flustered. We sprinkled water on her face but there was no reaction from the lady.

She had closed her locker and her bag was empty. It was apparent she had not come to collect anything from the locker that day. Perhaps she had come to deposit some items in her safe deposit box.

Kesavan and I somehow picked her up and carried her upstairs to the main hall where we laid her down.

Tremulously, I asked Kesavan, "Is she breathing at all?"

'Don't worry, sir. She's breathing. Let's admit her into the hospital next door. They'll treat her."

"Kesava, I'll stay here with her. Go and fetch a doctor."

The doctor examined her and recommended that we admit her into a hospital immediately.

"Doctor, what's wrong with her?" I asked in trepidation.

"I cannot conjecture, but it's imperative that she be admitted to a hospital immediately."

Kesavan and I arranged for Mrs. Chari to be admitted to the nearby hospital, relocked the bank's doors and stayed at the hospital with the lady. I also called up Mr. Chari and informed him of the situation.

I also called Gita and briefed her. She rushed to the hospital. After some first aid and intravenous drips, Mrs. Chari slowly opened her eyes and glared at me. Her look spoke volumes.

"How could you do this?" she asked angrily.

I had no answer. "I'm extremely sorry, Mrs. Chari. I assumed you had come out of the locker room."

She continued to glower at me.

In a private conversation, the attending doctor told me, "Good thing you found her when you did. An hour or two later, and it might have been 'goodbye Mrs. Chari'"

Those words shook me up. What a monumental error! Old Mr. Chari then arrived and started laying into me. I held his hands and sincerely apologised for my action, "It happened inadvertently. Please forgive me."

"I'll not let you off so easily. I'm going to the police," he said angrily. He was well-known to Gita and she pleaded with him to let me off this time.

Mrs. Chari was in hospital for two days and everyone from my bank's branch visited her and wished her a speedy recovery. My Chief Manager called me in to his room and roundly abused me.

"My branch has been defamed because of you."

Within two weeks of her discharge from the hospital, Mrs. Chari went about transferring all her accounts including the locker to Nanganallur.

My Chief Manager has written to our Regional Office recommending that I be transferred to some other remote branch in India.

(2014)

Dad's Favourite Newspaper

It was a Sunday in February, when I, Padmanabhan, was in Chennai, that dad met with his accident. Perhaps it would be better to characterise it as an 'incident' rather than 'an accident'. What should have been an ordinary everyday occurrence ended up as a serious matter. Dad is aged 83 and does not need glasses for reading his newspaper, watching TV or riding his bicycle. The last is an ancient model made in England. The old man had started out, all dressed up, to attend a wedding. My friend, Sibi Chelvan, encountering him in his finery had pulled his leg, "Watch out sir. People may mistake you for the groom!," causing dad to feel bashful.

A little later, while I was on the road, I received a call from my wife saying, "Dad has fallen off his cycle. Go and check on him immediately." She also mentioned his location and I rushed there straightaway.

Dad was seated in a chair in front of a house on the street and a small crowd had gathered round him. "He fell down when trying to get off the cycle," I was told by a member of the crowd. Dad clarified, "There was heavy traffic and I couldn't balance the bike and fell." I was very upset with him.

I rushed dad immediately to his regular doctor, Srinivasa Kannan. In actual fact, it was quite a feat getting him into an auto-rickshaw and ferrying him to the doctor's. He appeared to be in tremendous pain and even this simple act seemed beyond him. Srinivasa Kannan took one look at him and advised me, "Take him immediately to an orthopaedic surgeon," and wrote down the name and address of a reliable one.

I quickly took dad to the orthopaedic surgeon and an X-ray revealed a fracture in his hip. He was immediately admitted into the hospital by which time my brother had joined me. I was thankful it was a Sunday. Otherwise it would have been near impossible for me to get away from my workplace in the suburbs.

I did not get back to work till the operation was carried out and dad was discharged from the hospital. By this time, the officials at the bank where I was employed had succeeded in making my life quite miserable. Only persons who had gone through such an experience would feel the affected person's misery and empathise with him. But I seemed to be in the midst of insensitive creatures who had no consideration for others' feelings.

Once he was back home, the question arose 'who was to look after him?' Lakshmi offered to step in and help during the crisis. Dad ended up spending several weeks in bed. A strong person, he never stayed idle even for a second and was constantly moving his legs. While he was not napping, he would either watch TV or read the newspaper. His favourite daily was the *Dinamalar* and it was his habit to read it from end to end, column by column first page till the last. And, as I have mentioned, at age 84 he did not need his spectacles. Whenever I, Padmanabhan, mention this point, my wife would scold me, "Stop, lest the evil eye falls on him."

Dad would not merely read the newspaper but would also add his comments to the articles he read in it. When Jayalalithaa was in power, he would praise Karunanidhi's rule, and when Karunaninidhi formed the government, he would wax nostalgic about Jayalalithaa's efficient handling of affairs. Strange man!

One Sunday, I handed the paper to dad and asked him, "Dad, show me the article you are reading."

Dad perused the paper seriously and then lingered for a long time on one particular news item. He said to himself, "Good. So he's been caught at last. The rogue. It's about time." I took the paper from him to see which item of news he was commenting on.

The article completely threw me, for it was much more interesting than the mystery stories I used to devour. The story covered an entire page of *Dinamalar*.

I want you to also read the news item that dad and I read that day. Here is its condensed version:

The story came with several sensational headlines.

1,000 GOLD SOVEREIGNS, RUPEES 6 MILLION STOLEN!

THE 'BUREAU PULLING' THIEF NABBED AFTER SEVEN LONG YEARS!

HOW THE CASE WAS CRACKED - COMMISSIONER REVEALS ALL.

FROM MASON TO 'BUREAU PULLER'.

HE WAS A GRIP IN MOVIES!

RAID AT A LUXURY APARTMENT!

TWO FAKE ROBBERS ARRESTED TWICE!

THE 'SUPERSTITIOUS' ROBBER

Any one merely skimming the daily would find these headlines tantalizing enough to stop and read the full story.

Let's also examine the story.

A robber whose modus operandi was 'bureau pulling' and who had been eluding the entire police force for seven years had been finally nabbed. The thief, who had struck at over 200 places and robbed householders of 1,000 gold sovereigns worth of jewellery and 6 million rupees in cash in total, had fallen into the hands of the police almost by accident.

The 'bureau pulling' thefts first commenced in the suburbs of Chennai around the year 2000 and this novel method of robbery spread panic among the residents of outlying areas such as Adambakkam, Palavanthangal, Madipakkam and Nanganallur.

The thief apparently pulled cupboards containing cash and valuables towards a window noiselessly, and emptied them of their contents even while the residents were sound asleep inside their houses. This is what the police categorised as 'bureau pulling' thefts.

Initially, a special team under a Sub-Inspector was set up to nab the culprit. Even as this team was carrying on its hunt, a series of daring 'bureau pulling' thefts shook the city. Investigators were able to establish that a single person was behind all these robberies. Also, while there were a few fingerprints found at the scenes of some of the earlier crimes, the complete absence any trace evidence at later scenes was also proving a hurdle in establishing the identity of the perpetrator.

The police then made elaborate plans for arresting the culprit. A team of 200 policemen were deputed to the suburbs in 'mufti' led by 50 sub-inspectors. They were secreted on terraces of houses, tree-tops and other strategic spots to keep an eye out for any suspicious activity. A number of policemen also patrolled the streets in various vehicles and in different disguises.

Despite all these efforts, the 'bureau puller' eluded arrest. In February of 2004, he was spotted attempting to rob a house in Madipakkam, and a team headed by an Inspector gave chase. But he somehow managed to escape their clutches.

By matching the fingerprints found at that house with the previous ones, it was established beyond any doubt that it was indeed the 'bureau puller' whom they had foiled. Now, another team was formed under an Assistant Commissioner to nab him, but this squad too met with no success and was soon disbanded.

This elusive 'bureau puller' had accidentally fallen into the hands of the Madipakkam police the day before yesterday.

On that day, at around 8.30 p.m., a young man had alighted from a bus at Puzhuthivakkam bus stand.

Two policemen belonging to the Madipakkam police station were present there. When they noticed a flashlight in the man's hand, they grew suspicious.

They accosted him and asked why he was walking around with a flashlight in his hand. "I am visiting my sister," he replied and tried to walk away. On the basis of their suspicion, they took him along to the police station.

They took his fingerprints and compared them with that of the 'bureau puller', and discovered it was a perfect match. The stunned policemen immediately began their enquiries.

It transpired that the arrested man was named Nagamani and he was from Viluppuram. During the interrogation, Nagamani admitted that he was indeed the 'bureau pulling' robber.

What has been reported above is news, but it reads better than a thriller. Several reporters could have collaborated in putting this news together or just one person may have collated all the information. No names had been ascribed but every bit of the information was factual. Details of the robber's life story were conveyed under different headings, as we have seen above.

Under the headline "TWO FAKE ROBBERS ARRESTED TWICE", appeared the following story:

In March 2005, the police had arrested a thief named Kamalakannan and had claimed then that he was the 'bureau pulling' robber and that he carried out his activities in connivance with a policeman named Appadurai. But, unfortunately for them, neither's fingerprints matched those lifted at the various crime scenes of the actual 'bureau puller'.

To redeem themselves, the police then caught hold of an old lag, towards the end of 2006, and announced they had succeeded in cracking the case. It subsequently transpired that even though he had carried out robberies in at least four locations, his fingerprints did not match those of the 'bureau puller's' either.

The story under the heading "FROM MASON TO 'BUREAU PULLER'" was equally engrossing.

Nagamani told the police how he had come to Chennai to work as a mason and had become the 'bureau pulling' thief in course of time.

His confessional statement went as follows:

I hail from a small village near Gingee in Villupuram district. My father is a mason and I also trained as a mason.

Since employment opportunities were limited in my home town, I moved to Chennai in 2000 when suburbs such as Madipakkam, Puzhuthivakkam, etc. were developing very fast and many new buildings were coming up in these areas. I secured employment at several such new constructions and I used to spend the nights in these areas.

At nights, I used to spy on women sleeping in these buildings and on couples having sex.

It became routine for me to steal these women's handbags and wallets at such times. I also used to insert my hand through windows and pick up articles of value hung on the walls of houses. At one house, I opened up a cupboard which was near a window and stole all the jewels contained in it.

When I became aware that people stored their valuables in cupboards, I began targeting bureaus every night thereafter. In certain places, where the cupboards were located far away from the windows, I used a hook-like rod or a flexible hose to pull the almirah closer to the window and also poured oil on the floor to prevent any noise when it was being pulled. If, in the course of the operation, the bureau toppled over, I would immediately run away from the spot.

Back in my home town, I was in love with Selvi and later got married to her. When she saw I was flush with money, Selvi's sister, Jeeva, also fell into my snare and I took her as my second wife.

As my trade was proving to be highly lucrative, I was able to buy a house in Vijayaraghavapuram near Saligramam in Chennai, and moved in there with my wives. From the money I had stolen I was also able to pay a subscription of 45,000 rupees and join the Cine Technicians' Association and gain employment as a 'light boy' in movies. I have worked in several movies in this capacity and, on days when there was no shooting, I reverted to theft.

This was the gist of Nagamani's statement.

A titbit under the heading, "The SUPERSTITIOUS ROBBER":

Apparently, Nagamani was a mixture of superstitions and strange practices. Most of his robberies were carried out on Thursdays and it was his habit to approach the target house at 8:00 p.m. on those nights. He always carried a blade and a flashlight with him – the blade to cut open the mosquito netting on the windows and the torch to ascertain the location of the cupboard's handle.

Once he was certain that everyone in the house had gone to sleep, he would commence his operations at 11:00 at night. He wouldn't walk on two legs like the rest of us, but run on all fours very fast. Once the deed was done, he would saunter away casually from the spot.

The whole page of *Dinamalar* contained a lot more details about the 'bureau pulling' thief under various headings. In addition, his photograph had also been published.

When I finished reading the entire report, I asked dad, "What do you think of this news item?"

"Very bad. Shows the deterioration in the current law and order situation. We never had incidents like this during our times."

"Forget your times. Did you see how they have expanded this news item to cover an entire page and made it more interesting than a mystery story?"

"Whatever. It's still a piece of news. Tomorrow another sensational bit of news will supplant it, and people would forget this and move on."

"But I don't look at it simply as a piece of news. It seems to me there's enough source material here for an entire novel in the future."

"Really?"

"Several persons must have worked on this report. I am not sure if one person did the entire story or several reporters contributed to it. And Nagamani's confessional statement is also included in it. Considering the plot stratagems adopted in its telling, I consider this no less than a tale told in a postmodern style."

Dad didn't answer me as his attention had drifted to the television.

(2007)

The Double Decker Express

Last Thursday I travelled to Bengaluru by the Double Decker Express train. Since I was late in making my travel booking, it was the only train on which I could secure a seat. I was travelling to Bengaluru after a gap of nearly six years to meet up with a relation who was not keeping well. He is 79 years old and lives at an area called Malleshwaram in Bengaluru. He is presently having difficulty in locomotion, whereas in his prime no one could keep pace with his speed. Me, I am not so good at walking.

The facilities on the Double Decker train were dreadful. I found it difficult to fit my six-foot frame into one of its narrow seats. They had crammed three such seats close together and if all the three were occupied, 'uncomfortable' would be a mild word to describe the situation. Especially for the person occupying the window seat. If he needed to visit the toilet urgently, he would need to depend on the co-operation of both the other two passengers.

The toilet was worse than the seating arrangements. Its condition was deplorable and you needed to possess a strong stomach to even consider using it. The Indian Railways, which charges an exorbitant fare for the train travel, does not think it worthwhile to spend even a portion of it towards upkeep of the toilets. Every time you use the "facilities" you need to offer up a prayer to God to spare you from any contagious disease.

Braving all these odds I landed up at Bengaluru. The climate there was superb and I felt it was worth all the trouble to escape Chennai's heat and humidity.

My relative's house was a warren of small rooms and Malleshwaram itself seemed to be a pleasant but busy place with imposing showrooms. It appeared that every big brand in Chennai had its representation at Malleshwaram. The very first day I walked along Malleshwaram's streets I headed towards a large book store and bought "The Bible of Clay" for 50 rupees. It is by Spanish author Julia Navarro and I had long wanted to read it.

Besides, I am an avid collector of books, especially those being sold at sidewalk stalls at throwaway prices, where I am still able to bargain and haggle. Malleshwaram contained several such outlets.

When I returned home with the book, my relation asked me jokingly, "Did you come to visit me or to shop for books?"

"To visit you, of course. It's been such a long time since I was here last," I replied.

He was not in the habit of reading anything other than the daily newspaper. He would also occasionally watch TV. Because of his current illness, he only gives a cursory glance at the newspaper these days. He also struggles to eat properly as half the food drops off the spoon before he can get it to his mouth.

And to think, he used to be such an active person previously. He would go for long walks with absolutely no sign of tiredness. He did not even own a bicycle. He would also avoid auto-rickshaws wherever possible. He would only take the bus on occasions. I would find it difficult to walk around in Bengaluru because of its bumpy roads, full of ups and downs. Also, Bengaluru's climate encouraged laziness whereas in Chennai, despite its sticky heat, time seemed to fly.

"Because he knows he is adopted, Vishnu behaves like this with us," said the relative.

"This is his constant worry, apart from the fact that the boy does not seem interested in getting married," added his wife.

Both the days I was there, the boy was late coming back from work. He would have his meal and start chatting with friends on his phone till 11.00 at night when he would go off to sleep.

Apart from checking on the welfare of my relative, I thought perhaps I should give some advice to the boy regarding his marriage. But then, I thought to myself, "Who am I to advise him?" Apparently the boy did not like any of the girls proposed by his foster parents. He was my sister-in-law's third son and the two of them have raised him as their own. Everything was fine until he found out he was adopted. He had become incandescent with rage upon learning the truth. Some of the girls' parents hadn't helped matters exactly by wondering aloud why the boy's parents were so much older. Was he born to them late in their life, they would ask. Unwilling to dissemble, the parents would reveal the fact that he was their adopted son

The wife adds piteously, "We have grown too old and he seems to hate our very sight. He keeps going off to the corner shop to sneak a smoke."

I did not know how to console them. I was also surprised that adoption should produce such psychological issues.

Another day I called on two writer friends of mine who had moved to Bengaluru from Chennai. I was escorted to their home by another friend who was a resident of Bengaluru. I discovered that they had not changed a bit since I knew them. One of them was a critic and was in habit of tearing apart anyone he disliked. When I met him, he was talking caustically about an author I knew. Somehow I felt that they were both very lonely and unsettled still in Bengaluru. By the time I returned home to Malleshwaram after meeting them, it was quite late and a sense of disapproval was palpable in the household.

The husband and wife were too scared to discuss anything in the house while Vishnu was around, for fear it would lead to arguments and recriminations. Apparently he was in the habit of smashing things in the house when he was in a rage. So great was their dread of the boy, it was pathetic.

I was to leave on Saturday afternoon by the same Double Decker Express. In the morning, I took a walk in a nearby park.

Vishnu was sleeping when I left for my walk. Despite the late hour, they did not dare awaken him. I returned home quite late after my walk, and Vishnu was nowhere to be seen. When I enquired, they told me he had gone off to a mall with his friends. I was surprised. He did not return till the afternoon.

I took my leave after telling my relation to take proper care of himself.

"I only hope he gets married before I pass away," he said and I was saddened to hear the statement. I then proceeded to Bengaluru railway station and boarded the Double Decker Express for my return journey.

While I was in the train's upper level coming in, my seat this time was on the lower deck. But there was no improvement in the seating arrangement – I was once again trapped with no easy access to the toilet.

Near me, or, to be exact, in the seat in front of me, was a young girl aged around 20. She was reading an English novel and appeared very stylish. Her attire, however, stunned me. She had on a micro mini skirt and an expensive-looking top. The first thought that struck me was she would make an ideal match for Vishnu. While I did not want to be caught staring, my eyes kept returning to her from time to time.

But mainly it was her dress, or the lack of it, that bothered me.

In this train, it was no easy matter to push open the door to the compartment. You needed to push it with all your strength when it would open with a loud, complaining screech. I found it quite a strain trying to force the door open, while its shrill shriek set my teeth on edge.

Throughout the journey, vendors of different sorts would pass through the compartment hawking their wares, and they would be constantly pushing the door open providing me with no respite from its harsh squealing sound.

I felt that my over-aged sight was lingering too long on the girl in the miniskirt. While I felt it was unbecoming on my part, I could not help being bothered by the sight of her elegant body. 'Why was she travelling in such a costume?' I wondered. She appeared younger than my daughter and, if the latter had appeared in such skimpy attire, I would certainly have made her go back and change. I could not help but think that one of the main reasons for today's men losing self-control is the revealing clothes that modern girls sported.

To put an end to such thoughts I began leafing through the daily newspapers I had brought with me.

The girl in her micro mini skirt suddenly got up from her seat, went to the door and tried to open it. It was obviously tight and she tried forcing it open with all her strength, when something untoward happened. Her short skirt slid off her waist. At this she got flustered and, letting go of the door handle, she hurriedly re-adjusted it, looking around to see if anyone had noticed the 'wardrobe malfunction'. In particular, she gave me a piercing glance.

———

(2016)

The Patient

The room I was in contained 20 beds. All the occupants appeared woebegone as though they were nursing a secret sorrow. Everyone seemed to be suffering from some sort of unknown malaise. Our room was huge. My bed was next to a window. I could see lush, green trees through it. I wasn't aware what sort of trees they were. They had strange flowers festooned all over them every day. The chirping of birds kept us awake despite our physical discomfort. At least the trees provided a healthy environment.

A week ago, I was suffering from fever that just wouldn't go down. Appa began to worry. Amma initially offered to take leave of absence to look after me. And she did take time off for a week to nurse me. But my fever did not abate. Both of them then became worried. With no other option, dad asked my uncle to come and have a look. He is the officer in charge of the nurses at this government hospital. He got me admitted here. Dad comes around every evening and spends the nights with me at the hospital.

The very second day of my admission an incident took place here. The patient at the last bed at the end of my row was in a critical condition. They were administering oxygen to him. He was unconscious. Everyone was aware that the end was near. As he simply lay there comatose, the hospital authorities felt there was no point in trying to revive a man who did not respond to any treatment, and asked his relatives to take him home. When his family members came to collect him, they found he had passed away. All of them surrounded his bed and created a ruckus.

In quick time, that bed was cleared and presented a still, motionless appearance. I do not know what condition caused the man's death. But whenever my glance happened to fall on that vacant bed, it seemed to present a terribly menacing appearance. Every time I laid back and closed my eyes, I saw repeated visions of the dead man on his bed going through his last moments. Unwilling to display my inner fear, I pretend my fever has gone down and I am normal again. I began worrying that continuing to lie on the bed was a sign of prolonged sickness. I got off my bed and started walking around. The nurse in charge of the room looked up and asked me,

"Where are you off to, Hari?"

"Just stretching my legs."

"Don't strain yourself. You'll only aggravate your illness. Go back and lie down…"

At her stern tone of voice, unsure of my next course of action, I went and sat down in front of her.

She looked at me strangely.

"That man in the corner bed, he passed away!"

"So what?"

"No, nothing."

"We knew when he was being admitted that he wouldn't last long."

"How many patients die here?"

"Quite a few. You better get back to your bed."

I began moving away.

"Which Grade are you in?"

"Tenth."

I went and sat on my bed. The trees appeared to wink and laugh at me through the window. Two squirrels were busy chasing each other playfully. A flower drooped as though ready to fall off its stalk. I looked keenly at the patients around me. Most of them were dozing. One man was eating something. There appeared to be no possibility of forging any sort of relationship with any of them.

A hospital attendant came by. The nurse called him over and instructed him to clean the dead man's bed.

He picked up the rubber sheet from the dead man's bed and asked the nurse what he should do with it. She indicated my bed and told him to put it on mine. I was watching all this.

He brought the rubber sheet over to my bed. I felt an automatic sense of revulsion at the sight of it. Why should I use a dead man's rubber sheet? How can an item that recently supported a dead man's body be fitted onto my bed? I began keening loudly. The nurse came running at the sound and asked me what the problem was.

"I don't want this rubber sheet."

"Why? What's wrong?"

"It was earlier used by a dead man."

She looked at the ward boy and said, "Take it away. You don't need to put it on his bed."

At that, he took it away. I couldn't go to sleep until appa came by in the night. As soon as I saw him, I asked him to come over and sit beside me.

"What's the matter Hari?"

"The man at the end of this row died today."

"So what?"

"When can I go home? I don't like it here."

"Let's first concentrate on getting you better. Go to sleep now."

Saying this, appa went off to sleep himself. I was awake. I gazed at the stars through the window. The trees now presented a frightening appearance. In the darkness, they looked like frightful ogres dancing with wild,matted hair. I deliberately averted my eyes from the window. In the dim light, the room was silent. The night nurse was sitting at her station, half-asleep. In the silence of the night, the overhead fans could be heard creaking and groaning. I fell asleep despite myself.

In the morning they gave me a tablet along with a glass of water. After I had swallowed the pill, they gave me some tooth powder composed of salt to clean my teeth. I went towards the communal toilet. Their dental powder stung my mouth. Government hospitals need to take a note of this.

Morning routine and ablutions. I returned to my bed again. Appa was getting ready to leave. He needed to get home by seven thirty. This would give him enough time to shower and go to work. Amma had not come to the hospital even once since I had been admitted. She hates hospitals. Uncle was on duty at a different ward. But he always drops by to see me before he gets off duty. While leaving, he would request the nurse on duty to take good care of me.

It was through my uncle that I met nurse Leela. For some unknown reason, she showed me a lot of affection. She would sit on the stool next to my bed and talk for hours. Once we begin our conversation, I wouldn't realise the passage of time. Sometimes she would comb my disordered hair with her fingers. She would straighten my bed. I was naturally shy around girls. But as our interaction increased, I lost my innate shyness around Leela. When I saw her face at close range, I felt like kissing her on the cheek. Leela, of course, was older than me.

"When I see you, I'm reminded of my younger brother back home, " she said one day.

"Oh, really?"

"I live here all alone while my family is back in my hometown. I still feel very homesick."

"Does your brother resemble me?"

"You remind me so much of him. That's why I feel like chatting with you."

"Where does he study?"

"He goes to school just like you."

"Why did you leave them behind when you are lonely here?"

"It's only for a short while. I'll either go back to my hometown soon, or else bring them here to join me."

As far as she was concerned, it was sisterly affection. But I certainly did not feel very brotherly towards her. I experienced all the regular feelings and emotions when interacting with a girl. I even experienced inexplicable feelings of jealousy whenever I saw her talking and laughing with the male doctors in the hospital.

My situation returned to normal. I was now merely on pills. As an aftermath of the fever, my mouth felt bitter. My lips had turned dry and chapped.

"You're going home tomorrow," said Leela one Friday. My heart leaped with joy. She appeared sad.

Holding my hands, she asked, "Will you come back to see me?" I sat stunned not knowing what to reply. I simply kept staring at her face.

"You're very weak. Get the doctor to prescribe some good tonic. Take good care of yourself. If you come to see me, I'll be able to give you pills and boosters you require. Will you come?" I nodded my head.

"Every time I see you I get the satisfaction of seeing my brother back home."

As we were talking, another nurse came around to meet Leela.

"How come you're still here?"

"Hari is being discharged tomorrow."

She looked at me.

"I simply want to get out of this hellhole as soon as possible," I said.

"Why? What do we look like to you?" asked Leela.

"Pitiable…"

"I agree it could be irritating sometimes… some patients keep summoning us for no reason."

"Are you on the night shift next week?" asked the other nurse.

"Yes."

"Karunakaran will be on the same shift!"

"Oh my God!" exclaimed Leela.

"Who's Karunakaran?"

"You haven't met him. He's a doctor who's recently joined us. He's been after me ever since his arrival. That's what I am scared about."

"He has a weakness for women," explained the other nurse.

They then moved away still discussing the issue. I had fever the first day I landed here. Thereafter I had been fine. Life here appeared strange to me. The ever-present smell of disinfectant would continually assail your nostrils. And I had no other interaction with the rest of the patients. They were all older than me. Every evening, their beds would be surrounded by groups of relatives. The entire ward would be abuzz with their conversations with the patients. Generally, no one has ever come to meet me in the evenings. Sometimes, my uncle would drop in and take me to the hospital canteen and buy me idlis. Each day I would be praying for release from this miserable place.

Around five o' clock, the usual crowds had gathered around the various beds. A gentleman wearing sacred ash prominently on his forehead walked in and began dispensing the ash to every patient. When he came to me, I asked him, "What's this?"

"Prasad (religious offering) from the temple."

"Why are you giving it to us?"

"So all of you can be cured quickly...it's social service...I do this once a month," he said proudly.

The next day the doctors pronounced I could go home that evening itself. Appa was around when they said this and so he said he'd come back to take me home.

I was all ready to leave for home. Leela arrived. Since she was on night duty that day, she was still in her sari instead of her uniform. When she saw me, her eyes teared up and she held my hands affectionately.

"You won't forget, will you, Hari?" she asked, her voice breaking in emotion.

"No, I won't."

"Drop in and meet me on your holidays, if you can."

"Where will you be?"

"I'll be here in the ward. Otherwise at the hostel. That's also within this complex only. I'll give you the address."

She wrote down the details of her hostel and handed it to me.

"Who's taking you home?"

"Appa."

"Look after yourself...eat healthy food...you need to put on some weight...you are nothing but skin and bones now."

I was listening to her advice. Suddenly she hugged and kissed me. I began shivering in her embrace.

Appa came to fetch me. I took leave of her. As we walked out of the hospital, the loud roar of traffic assailed my ears. The city's walls were plastered with colourful posters advertising all the new movies showing at the city's various theatres.

———

(1988)

THE BLUNDER

It would be no exaggeration if I claimed that, as soon as I set eyes on Padma, I wanted to marry her and spend the rest of my life with her. She was tall and fair-complected. She wore glasses just like me. She initiated our friendship by complimenting me on my first published story. My first ever story had been published in a small magazine. Most of its hundred-odd subscribers were colleagues from my workplace. One day, Jagan called me on the intercom and asked me to come over to his department. From my desk on the second floor, I went up to his workstation on the fifth floor. That's where I met Padma. Her desk was right next to Jagan's. She had with her a copy of the magazine in which my story had appeared. Following a cursory introduction and a brief 'hello' to her, I began chatting with Jagan. I have no doubt he intuitively knew that I had not regained full control of my faculties following that brief introduction to Padma.

In the midst of our conversation, Padma suddenly remarked, "Your 'Sandal' is extremely good." I was a little taken aback and instinctively glanced down at my shoes. They were an old pair and nothing to write home about.

At that, Padma laughed and clarified, "I was referring to your story."

My shock turned into astonishment and I looked at her with a pleased smile on my face. I didn't see how I could have forgotten that the title of my story had been "Sandal"! While I felt I could have done a lot better as far as the story went, it had at least helped me secure Padma's friendship.

Two weeks after this episode, Padma came to my house. She brought along her maidservant with her.

In addition to it being the first time she was visiting me, bringing along a chaperone seemed to be an additional precaution on her part. Both our houses were in the same locality.

I invited her in and bade her sit. The maid stood at the threshold holding on to the door. I introduced Padma to my family members. I also offered her some coffee. Padma seemed to suddenly grow shy and I was looking at her disconcertedly.

"What brings you here so early in the morning?"

"I'm taking a few days off," she replied, handing me a leave application letter. She then kept looking all around the house as though to avoid eye contact with me.

"Where are you off to?"

"Something urgent has come up at our hometown and I need to go there immediately."

After finishing her coffee, as Padma was leaving, she thrust a story she had written into my hand.

"I'm very fond of writing. Please go through this and give me your opinion," she requested.

I accepted the manuscript from her as I rather liked the connection it established between the two of us. She then took her leave. I kept thinking of her the whole day.

Even after two or three days I had not begun reading her story. For, as soon as I received it, I had an inkling as to its nature. Some writings are like that. They wouldn't warrant even a cursory leaf through. You need experience to be aware of this. It is like some people who can evaluate a product in a shop merely by looking at it. Still, I felt I needed to go through the manuscript for Padma's sake. Her narration did not grip me. There was no skill in the story-telling. In spite of being an avid reader, she did not appear to have acquired the knack of constructing a proper tale.

I decided to meet Padma for the sake of her story at least. One day during lunch hour I called her on the intercom.

"I need to speak to you about your story."

"Where can we meet?"

"Can we meet at the café across the street?"

She seemed to hesitate.

"Is that a problem?"

"No, no. That's fine. Let's meet there," she agreed.

"Go ahead and grab a table. I'll join you."

The café was opposite our office. We seated ourselves in a secluded cubicle. I realised that neither of us was feeling comfortable with the situation. After placing our orders –

"So how was your trip?" I began on an artificial note.

"I didn't want to come back..."

"Why's that?"

"It was so very peaceful over there...meals at regular hours...lots of places to roam around in... sound sleep as soon as the head hits the pillow... no work worries or tension..."

"Wow, how I wish I had a place like that to go to…"

Padma merely gave a small smile at that remark and I was thunderstruck when I looked upon her smiling face. Inviting her to meet me at the restaurant was a bold step. Since this thought was playing on my mind, I was not my usual self. I was trying to play it safe. Padma was dressed very attractively and that further distracted me.

I was brought down to earth when she demanded, "Hey, where are you? Did you hear me…?"

"I'm sorry, you were saying…?"

"I was asking about my story."

"I'm sorry. My mind was elsewhere."

"I suppose all authors are like that."

"No, no. Not all authors are like that."

By then the food we had ordered appeared and silence reigned for a while. I could see Padma had long, slender fingers. Her finicky eating habits fascinated me.

"Your story could have been better."

Her face fell at that comment. Maybe I had been too abrupt.

As we were leaving the place, I handed her story back to her. The feeling I had experienced while receiving the story was not in evidence when it was being returned. But I did not feel like losing her friendship over this issue.

"I'm not yet experienced enough to judge another person's writing," I tried to explain.

I hoped these words would assuage her hurt feelings somewhat.

After this encounter, we did not meet each other for two to three weeks. The truth of the matter was that Jagan had spotted us as we were returning from the restaurant that day. I wished to protect myself against his snide comments. Padma too may have felt the same way.

One Sunday morning, I was making my way to the grocery store to get some butter when I happened to see Padma outside her house. Even though I knew her address, I had never attempted to drop in on her. It looked like she too was on her way somewhere.

"Would you like to come in?" she invited. I followed her inside without demur. She introduced me to everyone in her household. Including the maidservant who had accompanied her to my house. Padma seemed to have taken after her mother. The mother appeared more outgoing and friendlier than the father. She enquired all about my family and then went in to get me some coffee.

"Where are you off to, so early in the morning?" I asked Padma.

"To Computer class."

"Oh, did I upset your programme then?"

"Oh no! I was only going to enrol today. Would you like to join too? It's quite close to our houses."

I thought about it. This was a golden opportunity. I could not keep meeting Padma at our workplace. Jagan would be around. The Computer classes sounded ideal for meeting her regularly and provided a good enough excuse.

Both of us enrolled for the Computer course. I found out the time she left home daily for the classes and managed to arrive at her street corner exactly at that time seemingly by happenstance. We would then proceed together to the classes. Within a few days this became a routine and she began to anticipate my arrival.

One morning she was not around. She was missing from the class as well. I bumped into her on my way back home.

"You were absent from class today?"

"My marriage is being fixed."

I stood there stunned and speechless. I was shell-shocked. Worried that my silence might be misconstrued, I simply said, "Congratulations", and quickly took leave of her.

I couldn't sleep that night. I sat alone in the terrace and listened to Ananda Shankar's songs. Sadness overwhelmed me. I felt something valuable had slipped away from my grasp. At that stage I began imagining improbably wild scenarios. I envisioned Padma suddenly developing an incurable heart condition and her fiancée refusing to go through with the wedding as a result. As she sheds bitter tears at this unexpected turn of events, I appear in front of her. Wiping her tears away, I gallantly offer to give her a new life. What nonsensical thoughts!

After this episode, I avoided meeting Padma. And, within a short while, my Computer classes also tapered off. In reality, the computer stuff went right over my head. Our office was a huge seven storied structure with thousands of employees and we worked in different corners of the building. One day I received a call from her.

"Why haven't I heard from you?"

"When's the wedding?"

"Oh, that's still four, five months away."

I grew predictably silent. This was happening to me regularly as a matter of course. As soon as the thought of her impending marriage would strike me, I became mute.

"Why are you quiet?"

"No…it's nothing…"

"Did you fall into a reverie again?"

"Oh no, it's nothing like that…"

"Have you written anything else subsequently?"

"No, I haven't."

"Amma wanted to meet you… apparently she's has something to talk to you about…"

I wondered why her mother wanted to talk to me.

"All right then…I'll hang up…"

"Wait…don't get upset Padma…I'll come and meet your Amma."

"When?"

"I'll come tomorrow itself…"

But I couldn't make it the next day. Without fail, Padma called up once again.

"We were expecting you…"

"Sorry, something urgent came up. Shall I come on Sunday?"

She disconnected without a further word. Perhaps she was angry with me. Why does her mother want to see me?

At around ten on Sunday morning, I went to Padma's house. Her mother answered the door. She invited me in smilingly and offered me a seat. Padma came out to greet me looking dewy fresh from a shower with her loose hair flowing. I was stunned for a moment when I looked at her. The familiar feelings began to rear their head again.

"Get Shankar some coffee..." her mother instructed Padma.

Padma vanished into the house in what seemed to me a flash of lightning. Her mother then proceeded to relate stories about Padma from her childhood to the present day, backed up by photographs. Padma looked horrible in her childhood pictures, appearing thin and lanky in every one of them. In the pictures of the three of them together, at least one of them would invariably appear awkward – looking like the odd one out. The mother went on with other exploits of Padma and I sat there listening to her and wondering where all this was leading to. Padma came out beaming and bearing coffee. As I again gazed at her in total bewilderment, an indescribable feeling of desolation swept over me. I was scared I might fumble and drop the coffee mug when I accepted it from her hands. What was lost was lost. It was my fault that I had failed to indicate my interest in her even indirectly. But, by the same token, couldn't Padma have signalled her intentions, during the intervening period?

"I understand you write stories?"

I merely smiled shyly at the mother.

"Have your works been published?"

"Yes. But not in the magazines you normally read."

"Where do they appear then?"

"Mostly in small magazines."

"Amma, his story *Sandal* was very good."

"Padma showed it to me. But I didn't understand it."

"That's no big deal."

I thought I should take my leave. The conversation was getting me down. Also, Padma's appearance and proximity were affecting me.

Padma's dad, who had gone out, returned home. I greeted him smilingly though I felt hypocritical about it.

"Padma's husband-to-be is a distant relation of mine."

Without looking at her, I could sense Padma blushing at this statement. I felt the time had come for me to leave the place. It seemed to me that every additional moment I spent there I was losing my self-control. Perhaps her mother understood how I was feeling. For she then unexpectedly addressed me saying,

"My dear child…"

I was aware she worked as an English teacher in a nursery school. However this form of address jolted me. I stared at her uncomprehendingly.

"I don't know what we are going to do about Padma's wedding. It's going to be a very expensive affair."

Now I finally understood her mother's intention in addressing me in that fashion. Perhaps I anticipated this from the beginning. I kept quiet.

"Please don't misunderstand me. I look upon you as a son. Padma told me that you have lost your mother…Padma has always been a clever girl right from childhood…I need your help…I need you to somehow let me have fifty thousand…I know you don't have it readily on hand…But Padma says that if you register yourself in the Benevolent Association at your office, you could raise this amount as a loan…Padma will pay it back in monthly instalments on your behalf…if both of you enrol into the Society, you can mutually assume responsibility for each other's loan…since you are both in the same office, the procedure should be easy enough…"

I kept quiet.

"I don't expect you to tell me your decision straightaway. Think about it, take a week's time and let us know," said the mother seemingly exhausted by her speech.

As I left their house, one fact struck me. Throughout all this her father had not said a single word to me. Padma accompanied me to the doorway.

"Please give the proposal your careful consideration Shankar."

"I will," I said and took myself away.

Approximately a week later, Padma came to see me at my place of work. My family members did not want me to take loans from the Office Society. They also warned me against getting involved in such matters.

"My family members are against the proposal," I said.

As soon as she heard this, Padma got up and left the place without another word. I felt uncomfortable. I was now the target of anger of a girl I liked a lot. But I also felt I was in the right. If I took a loan from the Society, not only would a substantial chunk of my salary go every month towards its repayment, but I could also be stuck with Padma's loan amount if, for any reason, she defaulted.

Though I felt bad the whole day, I bounced back to normalcy very soon. I did not see Padma for a number of days thereafter. I didn't take any special efforts to meet with her either.

The next time I saw Padma was when she came around to give me her wedding invitation. I was a bit disappointed as I had hoped she would come home to hand it to me personally. Instead she gave it to me at the workplace, along with the rest of the colleagues. As she handed the invite over to me, she mouthed the words, "Please do come" exactly like she did to all the others. Her body language and facial expressions were those of a person meeting a stranger for the first time in her life. It was obvious that she was deliberately cold shouldering me.

I kept obsessing about her long after she had left the place. She had obviously still not forgiven me for not having raised the loan for her marriage. Perhaps she had not expected that from me.

Still, I decided I would attend her wedding. The hall where her marriage was scheduled to be held was also in our locality. I have been living at the West Mambalam area since my childhood for approximately 20-odd years now. Twenty years back, this suburb was not a very salubrious place to live in, to put it mildly. There were no proper transport facilities. The marriage hall mentioned in the invite was probably located somewhere near my old apartment building (we live in our own house now). For ages that was the only wedding hall I knew of in the locality.

The place was totally transformed now. There was a proper asphalted road and vehicles were whizzing around freely. It was still very congested. There were a lot of new buildings. There were also a number of shops around for the convenience of the residents. Chemists' shops and hospitals seemed to dominate. It suddenly appeared to be a new and competitive environment. There was an open ground where I used to play cricket with my schoolmates. A huge school stood in that place now. At the spot which used to serve as a makeshift gym for people to exercise, night cricket games are being held. That spot also serves as a venue for political rallies. The street adjoining the railway station used to be impassable during the rains as it used to be covered with slush. That narrow street also used to be perennially crowded. They have now removed the shops on either side of the street and widened it somewhat.

I didn't want to take the whole day off for Padma's wedding. I left my house early in the morning. I had already informed my office that I would be an hour late coming into work that day. Since the *muhurtam* (auspicious moment) for the wedding was very early in the day, I was unable to reach the hall in time for it.

When I arrived at the hall, there were very few people around. Empty chairs greeted me. Two young girls standing at the entrance sprinkled rose water on me. I touched the sandalwood paste with my fingers as a formality and entered the hall. A man approached me and smilingly welcomed me saying, "Hello sir. Come in, come in…" I walked in with him. He led me directly upstairs to the dining hall where some 20 to 25 persons were eating breakfast. I could see no familiar faces among them. I assumed no one from the office had arrived yet and mentally kicked myself for turning up so early. The gentleman accompanying me led me to a table and seated me.

I was unable to fully comprehend the state of my mind at the wedding. I was of course disappointed that it was not taking place between me and Padma as I had originally hoped for. But, even if such an event had taken place, would Padma still have transformed into a selfish person expecting something in return for the relationship? The changes I noticed in her behaviour after I announced my intention of not availing the loan from the company were distressing, to say the least. As far as I was concerned, the feeling I started with of being willing to do anything for her sake had slowly evaporated from my mind as soon as it was clear she was not destined for me. I was still ambivalent about seeing her in her bridal finery.

I felt I should catch a quick shufti and leave the place. Fortunately, her mother had still not hove into view. Everyone else around looked unfamiliar. I didn't recognise even one of them.

I went down after breakfast. The gentleman who had escorted me upstairs was waiting.

"Where is the couple?" I asked and he took me inside. I was both eager to see Padma and feeling apprehensive about it at the same time. When I looked up to catch a sight of her, I stopped as though I had stepped on a live wire. What I saw was not Padma, but an old couple. Smiling, with garlands around their necks, they presented an ugly sight to my eyes. They smiled when they saw me approaching. I stopped not wishing to go near the couple. How did this mistake occur? I immediately came out of the hall. I appeared to be having palpitations. I plopped myself down on a chair when the gentleman who had escorted me to the dining hall came over. I hid my real feelings and gave him a weak smile.

"Have you paid your respects to the couple?"

I merely nodded. He went away satisfied. The crowd I had seen at breakfast was milling around.

My immediate worry was how to quietly escape from that place. But that persistent gentleman was still around, standing only a short distance away. I needed to evade his scrutiny and make a getaway. He however seemed rooted to his spot. In my agitation, I felt he was keeping his eye on me. I needed to quietly sidle away from the hall. What a mess! The fellow however showed no signs of moving away from his spot. As I furtively glanced at him from time to time, it seemed he was doing the same to me. I needed to use all my wits to get out of this situation before anyone realised I had gate-crashed the wrong wedding ceremony.

As he turned his head away for a moment, I quickly got up from my chair. But, as soon as he saw me standing up, he came running towards me. Both of us exchanged meaningless smiles.

"None of my friends have turned up yet..." I said generally.

"Oh, is that so?"

"I'll go up to the front and look for them."

"Sure. Go ahead."

I came up to the gate. He stood steadfast in his place. As soon as I reached the road, I began strolling aimlessly as though looking for someone and, as soon as I crossed the wedding hall, I speeded up. My actions induced laughter within myself. As soon as I reached the main road abutting the hall, I turned and gave a quick look back. No one was paying me any attention. I was able to relax only after the hall disappeared behind me.

I then fished out Padma's wedding invitation from my pocket. It mentioned a different street altogether. I was surprised to learn that another new wedding hall had sprung up in the locality. As far as I knew, the only hall in the area was the one I had landed up in that morning. I was very sure of it.

When I entered the building named in the invitation, I realised that a house belonging to one of my old schoolmates had been transformed into a marriage hall. I had made the mistake of not noticing the Street name. Neither had I paid any attention to the name of the wedding hall.

The hall was very crowded. A lot of our office colleagues were present. Padma's mother was visible in the distance speaking to someone. There was nobody at the entrance to welcome the guests. I could see Padma. She was shimmering in a silk sari.

One of my colleagues spotted my arrival.

"Have you had your breakfast?"

"Yes."

"But I saw you walk in just now. When did you eat breakfast?"

I realised I had been caught out and mumbled, "At home, before I started out."

I pushed my way through the crowd and went and stood in front of Padma. She introduced me to her husband. I smiled and shook his hand. Padma looked gorgeous in her silk sari. The crowd began heaving behind me. In the melee I was pushed along and out of Padma's line of vision. I started to leave the venue. No one enquired after me or urged me to stay for lunch. Padma's mother was still busy talking to some guests. Even though I was within her range of sight, she obviously did not remember me. When I reached the doorway to the hall, someone handed me a wedding gift bag. I grabbed it and walked quickly towards the office.

February 1990

About the Author

Several selected poems of Azhagiyasingar have been translated into English and he continues to pen stories, poems and essays. Four of his short story collections – *Sila Kadaigal* (A Few Stories – 1991), *406 Chathura Adigal* (406 Square Feet – 1997), *Ram Colony* (2005) and *Roja Nira Chattai* (The Pink Shirt – 2013) – have so far been published. Similarly, three of his essay collections and four anthologies of poems have also been released. To his credit also goes the 2017 essay collection titled *Thirantha Puthagam* (Open Book). His short story *Uncle* fetched him the prestigious Katha award in 1998. His translation of Irawati Karve's *Yuganta* also won him the esteemed Thirupur Tamizh Sangam's award. His poems and stories have been translated into English, Hindi and Punjabi.

He continues his association with several literary magazines. Single-handedly and steadfastly he has been publishing the Tamil Literary Quarterly *Navina Virutcham* for the past 34 years.

Having retired from the services of a nationalised Indian bank, after 36 years, he lives in Chennai with his wife. He is 66 years old and has a daughter and a son.

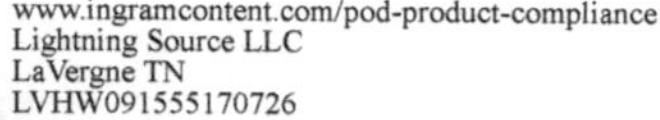

9 789390 053094